# THE BURIAL GROUND

# THE
# BURIAL
# GROUND

*A Novella*

## PAULINE
## HOLDSTOCK

1991
NEW STAR BOOKS
VANCOUVER

New Star Books Ltd.
2504 York Avenue
Vancouver, B.C.   V6K 1E3

Printed and bound in Canada by Hignell Printing
using chlorine-free, PH-neutral paper
1 2 3 4 5   95 94 93 92 91
First printing, October 1991

The author is grateful for assistance provided by the Ontario Arts Council.

The publisher is grateful for assistance provided by the Canada Council and by the Cultural Services Branch, Province of British Columbia

In writing this book, the author consulted a number of memoirs and journals. One work which proved particularly useful was *Mission to Nootka*, edited by Charles Lillard. *The Burial Ground* is nonetheless a work of fiction and is peopled wholly with characters of the author's imagination.

**Canadian Cataloguing in Publication Data**

Holdstock, Pauline, 1948–
   The burial ground
   ISBN 0-921586-25-6

   1. Indians of North America—British Columbia—Pacific Coast—Fiction. I. Title.
PS8565.0622B8 1991      C813'.54      C91-091682-9
PR9199.3.H64B8 1991

THE BURIAL GROUND

# I

THE PRIEST

Mrs. Hammond, impressive in some dark shiny stuff, getting up to speak, the Bishop removing his glasses, patiently resigned while the ladies have their say. Father Lawrence rudely blowing his nose as Mrs. Hammond begins.

I should remember this luncheon. There may not be another like it for—what? A year? Years? And yet isn't that just what I'm escaping from, the jellied veal and the pies packed with good works, the little cakes, "We knew you'd like these, Father, your favourites"? All the smiling ladies with their souls squeezed tight in their corsets and the husbands with their lusts only just concealed.

Father Lawrence, now, he would hang on to his jellied veal at all costs. What would it take to make him give it up, any of it? More than the chance to run his own parish on some fir-bristled knuckle of land punched into the edge of the Pacific. Where the congregation would not understand a word he said.

Mrs. Hammond concluding, reaching for the morocco-bound book that Mrs. Petit has been holding like a pane of glass since the tea was served.

"And with our blessing, Father,—" Now the Bishop staring straight at her as if her audacity is bursting from her bodice.

"And with our blessing, Father, accept this token," and she puts the palm of her hand flat on the book, swearing her sincerity, "of our wholehearted support."

Some wholehearted tapping of fingers on palms. "Hear, hear!" from Father Lawrence rummaging in his cassock for another handkerchief. But she has not finished.

"May you return with a true and praiseworthy account, one of which we may all in this diocese feel justly proud."

A little, awkward silence. Are they waiting to see if she has finished or are they all, under their bonnets, heading up the godforsaken coast themselves, piping encouragement to each other across the dangerous water, nodding from the darkness under the teetering pines?

"And may God go with you." Oh yes. Oh yes, Mrs. Hammond. May God indeed.

I take the book—this gift suggested by the Bishop who knows I will not write—say some things about doing it justice, keeping faith; they laugh obligingly. But I do not want their tokens of support or their blessings—firearms maybe or some lumber and nails, a keg or two of Mrs. Burcy's home-brew—but no tokens please. Least of all this blank journal. To record for their edification, perhaps for their entertainment, how I succeed or fail in my contract with my God. To receive their hopes and their expectations is to go trammelled. The blank pages are eyes agape, ears open to hear how I redeem myself.

But I take it. If the Bishop wants a journal, the Bishop shall have one. Bishop's pawn indeed. For just a little while longer.

## THE GIRL

Listen. This story begins before the time of the Father-not-father.

There was once an Old Woman of great power of the clan of the Eagle. Of her children only two survived, a daughter and a son. To the daughter was due the Old Woman's title and all her wealth and so in the way of the people had it been for five generations. From the mother to the daughter.

As soon as she was a woman, the daughter married a young man of fabulous wealth. His blankets and his feast dishes were without number. They passed to his wife. The young woman and the man of fabulous wealth were happy—and then the strangeness began.

At first it was nothing more than a thickening, a redness to the skin about the face and neck of the young man, the fabulously wealthy. A shaman was summoned. The shaman grew rich; the skin thickened more. Loosened now and sagged in folds and wrinkles, it was a vile drapery pinned here and there by hardened kernels of flesh.

The Old Woman was mad with shame for her daughter, her heir. She sent the young man out into the forest. To fast, she said. And her daughter went into mourning.

From time to time the young man returned like a sick dog that will not be beaten away. Each time he returned, his affliction had worsened until his jowls and throat were covered over with the reddened flaps and droplets of flesh; and yet each time he stayed a little longer than the time before, until finally he would not be sent back but lay behind the Old Woman's house where the daughter would peer at him mournfully through the cracks in the houseboards, and would come to him—when there was no moon—with scraps of food.

At last a house, a hut, was built for him at the far end of the village. When the last roofboard was knocked into place, the young man got up, went into the Old Woman's house that he had not entered in eighteen months, took his wife by the hand and led her away—and not all the coppers and cooking pots, blankets, knives and trinkets that the Old Woman had garnered could stop him.

From that moment, his flesh halted its creeping under his skin, but the damage was done.

He bought himself a slave, a girl child, and the young woman his wife remained childless.

Now see the Old Woman furious. She was without heirs. She hauled out her treasure again, increased the brideprice to rehusband the daughter. But no one came forward. And, stranger still, the daughter, had an offer been made, would have refused.

And this, too. Listen. A sealing party out at night. The Old Woman's second child, her son, and his wife, a Raven woman, were with them.

But this wife, the daughter-in-law, was unclean. She bled still from the birth of an idiot babe, a limp and vacant thing that she had left in the scrawny arms of its sister.

★

And so I, the Girl, am left to wait at home with this infant, my brother, and my dreams are all of bloated heads. In the morning, all but one of the boats returns.

For three weeks the Girl's dreams rocked, swollen in the surf until the bodies of her parents nudged the sand of a small island in the narrows.

The Old Woman mourned briefly.

Now she saw a way to continue the line of the Eagle. She gave a great feast at which much treasure was divided. At this feast she declared the young girl and the slack-limbed infant to be formally adopted by their aunt and uncle, her own childless daughter and the wattle-necked husband. The two children, she said, relinquished their place in the clan of the Raven and assumed all titles and wealth due to them in the Eagle line.

In this way, the Old Woman repossessed her grand-daughter and acquired her Eagle heir. The Girl's elder sister, a Raven child newly married to a brooding, sullen man, did not protest, having obsessions of her own.

For her interference, the Old Woman paid five hundred blankets, four hundred pelts, and two slaves to those who would have had it otherwise.

And so the Girl and the idiot babe lived in the house of the childless couple. But the aunt sickened. She grew tired of the sight of the pig-eyed, snuffling baby, tired of the vision of the bloated bodies of her drowned brother and his wife. And in the night when she opened her eyes and saw under her still lids the thick body of her husband straddling the Girl, and the Girl's mouth calling soundlessly, it was enough.

One night she left the house and did not return, and although her canoe was found, her body did not return to the stones.

★

Now I, the Girl, am left with the idiot child and the monstrous man. The Girl's fear of the man is very great, so great that she can tell no one. Shout it across the noisy creek where they pick the slivers of fish from the nets? Whisper it under the listening trees? It is not possible. To tell it is to set it loose like a madman in the woods, unpredictable. But, worse, the Beautiful Boy of her own village, and for whom she longs, will hear it trampling her honour and will hold himself aloof from her forever. She can not tell her sister, who lies with her Sullen Man and whose thoughts are all of another in the darkness; least of all can she tell her grandmother, the Old Woman—who will choose not to believe.

And so, instead, the Girl at night slipped under the blanket where the baby was sleeping like a blind puppy. She held the warm body and rubbed the flat nose with her lips, and closed her eyes, wishing she could crawl into the baby's sleep, away from the man, her uncle, with his choking, strangling snore.

And sometimes, not having any other way out of her trouble, she tried to dream a way out. She dreamed of the Beautiful Boy that she wanted for hers, but he remained remote and beautiful like a coloured bird under water; she dreamed of the White Shaman that they said would come, white like an aspen or the stem of a birch, who would cross the water like a heron wading. But in her dream the Girl could always see his feet, and they ended in claws. The claws gripped each wave and shook it free. Ribbons of red trickled down the clear green slopes of water and the shadows of his arms were in the shape of the thunderbird.

And so in her unhappiness the Girl continued to fear the man and love the child, to long for the Beautiful Boy and to wait for the White Shaman.

## THE PRIEST

*In The Year Of Our Lord One Thousand, Eight Hundred And Sixty*
*12TH NOVEMBER    Came ashore at our chosen land yesterday at 11 o'clock, after a satisfactory tour of the more northerly villages. The sheltered SW aspect of this site, its accessibility, & above all the hospitable nature of its people (features we have already noted in our preliminary reports last March) all conspire to make it the perfect home for our mission. (That it will remain so is ensured by the mutually beneficial agreement settled with the Chief last March, which not only secures approval for the mission but further provides us with lands & labour requisite for the establishment of the same.)*

And such a sight it was. Mats all over the beach. Blankets all over the housefronts. Laundry day with the Redman, Father Lawrence said. All the villagers gathered in front of the houses up on the high ground, pulling their cloaks round themselves against the wind. The men in the canoe barely decent. Not to be described for Mrs. Hammond and her ladies at home. Just some kind of scrap hanging down in front but nothing between them and the weather behind. They must have been freezing. The first mate said the grease keeps them warm. I don't know what it is but I can still smell it on me from their bodies as we sat crammed in the canoe.

Not built for men of my height. I could hardly get up when we came near the shore and then two of them had to steady me, keep me upright. Christ's envoy... The other men used their paddles to slow us down. And we waited. And they waited. Every man and woman in the village up there on the high beach in front of the longhouses. All quiet they were, stock still. Only the tops of the tall trees moving, and my cassock snapping out behind me in the wind. There wasn't a sound from them until I raised my arms. Then what an uproar. Stamping and shrieking to raise the dead. Easy now to say I rather think they liked the gesture. "Dear Christ," said Father Lawrence, and it sounded more like blasphemy than prayer.

*A spirited welcome greeted our arrival,*

And then there they were, charging down on us like savages. Howling. Poor old Lawrence, just stepping over the side, one leg in and one leg out, turned quite pale, I thought. Evidently couldn't decide whether to carry on or put the first leg back in the boat. But it wouldn't have done any good, climbing back in. Not if they'd really meant business.

*followed by a cordial address from the Chief.*

Who was as much at a loss as we were, it seemed, in all the confusion. He stood on the high ground for a moment, his hands outspread. In welcome it might have been. Or as if something ran like water out of his grasp.

But he put the best face on it, came down the red carpet affair they had rigged up with mats, planted himself square in the front of us and started making speeches.

A match for the Bishop even—if we only knew what on earth he was saying. I caught Lawrence looking askance. Clearly not prepared to credit this old brown man like a piece of tree come to life with his great cedar cape and his hair all strung with feathers and with shells. And the words might have been bird calls for all we could make of them. The translator we brought with us—the one L. calls the mynah bird—in his full suit of clothes and with his hair tied in a brush over his forehead, chipped in every now and then. But his word here and his word there surely bore no sensible relation to the verbal deluge from the Chief. Support for L.'s assertion that the man is making it up to please himself. But we have to at least try to trust him, hope that the truth will come to us, one way or another. We don't have any choice.

Father Lawrence began to mutter. "He's telling you his life's story, that's what he's doing. We could be here until the resurrection of the dead at this rate."

Unlikely that his patience would last that long, I thought. His manners might well have put us out of our misery sooner than he expected, and in a most unwelcome manner. So I took a chance and stepped forward and stuck out my hand.

As an indication of goodwill it seems not the best gesture to make in these parts. The Chief stopped talking all right, but the silence was not easy.

He looked from one to the other of us, his mouth turned down so far he might have been near to grief, and then he smiled and offered both his hands.

*Immediately following which, we were conducted to the lodge,*

★

The huge longhouse, a barn of a place, filled like a warehouse, crammed to the rafters with their belongings: weapons, tools, baskets, slings and nets. Not a post or beam anywhere but it wasn't festooned with blankets, branches, fish drying, meat curing, pelts, pots, even poultry, or something that looked rather like, hanging upside down in a corner. And in another corner, fantastic images in painted wood, like stage properties, grimacing and stuck with hair. But the floor. It was not as I'd expected—all white with crushed shells. It may even have been laid for our benefit. The best table linen.

*where we were feasted and honoured with a greater degree of respect than we have previously encountered anywhere on this coast.*

I could tell them of course about the war knives. It's what they hope to read. And expect. Only eight miles north of here. No canoe out to meet the schooner so we took the long boat with a couple of crew. The entire village had assembled on the beach. To greet us, we thought. Waving.

And then the canoe came at us from the shelter of some rocks.

Father L. unable, without his glasses, to see the knives, or that two of them had muskets, asking "What's that they're carrying?" But he didn't get much of an answer. I was too busy screaming at the 2nd mate. "Get out of here, man!" I've never seen a body turn a boat so fast in my life. He took one look over his shoulder at the shore and spun her round like a top. Rowed back as if the very devil were after us. Which is not too far off the mark. I took Lawrence's pistol and fired twice into the air and they held off—the canoe sitting

there, their leader standing in the prow, a knife raised,
challenging us to shoot at him. And Father Lawrence,
God forgive him, Father Lawrence urging me to do it,
"Now's your chance, man! Now's your chance."

Yes, I could tell them. It is what they expect.

And our next reception, three miles on. Word travels
faster than a peal of thunder here. It was eerie. Enough
to make your skin creep, thinking about it. Rowing
into that little cove, the water all still and no noise
coming from the village, like rowing out of the world.
Nothing. No sign of preparation, no sign at all of life.
No blankets, no nets, no canoes even. And not a solitary human figure. Cold.

It isn't any wonder Lawrence was taken with apo-
plexy when we finally got here and they all began to
yell. But afterwards, the relief! To see at last the place
all ready for us. Thrones, if you please, erected at the
end of the room. Old boxes covered over with skins.
But welcome. Welcome.

And timely, too, because there were more speeches
at the feast. And more. Two hours of them, Father L.
said. He was timing them. And a new dish for every
speech. God knows what they all were. Everything
plastered with grease and it all seemed to be fish.
Dried, mashed, whole, baked, frothed up. You'd
think they'd tire of it. I tried to look hearty, but Father
L. wasn't eating—thinking about the beans and salt
pork Captain Brinks said would be waiting back on
board.

*After many more speeches we performed the blessed work of*
*John and baptized almost 20 souls.*

It was a risk, interrupting them a second time. No one
murmured when I stood up. How do you gauge a

silence? By the hairs on the back of your neck? But there was nothing else for it, only get on and hope for the best. I told them the captain had to sail on the evening tide—not quite the whole truth, but for the sake of Our Lord...

I said we would have time before Father Lawrence sailed to do the tribe the honour of baptizing their infants. Then the mynah bird was at a loss for words. I explained it carefully, simply enough I thought. But some things don't bear translation. He looked doubtful, kept frowning, pulling his shirt-cuffs out of his sleeves as if the answer might come out written on them in India ink. And at last he had it: "*Wash-filthy-spirit-holy-name-ceremony.*" Not the most felicitous choice. The old people would have nothing to do with it but went off, grumbling. Somebody spat. We would have been lost were it not for the Chief—and whatever made him come forward, moved him to say yes.

The whole company moved outside then. Thank God. To be outside in the open air. I cannot stand their dark barns. Such a press of bodies...smells...darkness. And something more. It is what I fear most, a presence in a Godless place. I feel closed in with it, deserted, even with another white man beside me. Jesus Christ is with us. And yet...God forgive me. I know Thou art in all places always by my side. And the spirit of the Holy Ghost will not desert me. Ever.

But what a long and tedious time we had to wait for any of them to come forward. The Chief took us to a great cedar dugout trough and his slaves, hardly more than children, drew fresh water for us to bless. Only they made such a performance of it that most of the villagers skulked off.

By the time we had it done there was no one left, only faces at doorways. And in the cracks of the houseboards too, I shouldn't wonder. Dogs snuffing round and a crow insistent and cross up on one of the poles. A mockery, really. But we waited. Dear Lord it grew cold, too, when the sun went down behind the trees.

And yet it was a sight to marvel at. The village all quiet, a thin mist coming in off the sea, the shadows from the big trees running lenten purple over it all.

But lonely, waiting...

Lawrence was quiet. He had the case open and the pistol was in there along with the holy vessels and I knew what he was thinking: ambush. There was nothing of the kind, thank God. Only the girl, coming out of the shadows.

I couldn't make out what we were seeing at first. She walked out so immeasurably slowly with the great overgrown baby dangling against her own thin body. You could tell there was something wrong even from a distance. Its head so huge, hanging so unnaturally, too. Strange that it should have been the first one, poor thing. Lips slack, wet. Tiny little eyes, blank. It made no response to my face, not a frown, not a smile, nothing. The girl herself had her eyes fixed on me, like a calf under the knife. She was ready to run. I shall not forget the face in a hurry.

Or the moment, the beginning of my ministry.

But the language is no help. Heaven knows when I'll get the hang of it. Chinook serves us for now, but their own language is an abomination. I can't even get my tongue round some of the words they tell me.

"*Poor-baby-with-head-big-like-bladder*": the mynah bird's translation of the idiot baby's name. What a degradation for one of God's creatures. I told them it would never do.

"'*Thomas*'," I said. "We shall call him 'Thomas.' Yes,

that will do very well." (Of course Father Lawrence afterwards wouldn't believe me, but it had in all honesty slipped my mind for a moment: Father Thomas Lawrence.) I don't know whether I convinced the girl. She looked dubious. But then so did Father Lawrence.

As he felt in the case for the phial of chrism, he kept looking over to the houses; he had his glasses on this time. He's not trusting enough. I told him on the way back if we were going to be murdered they could have done it a hundred times while we were waiting. All the same. . .

He unstoppered the chrism and I traced the cross on the child's forehead. The skin was as smooth as vellum. I took a cup of water. Some of the people moved closer. "I baptize thee Thomas, in the name of the Father, the Son, and the Holy Ghost." And praise God, the child didn't cry. I knew then why the Lord sent us this imbecile who registered neither pleasure nor pain.

And I could not have prayed for a better witness than the girl. For the first time she breathed easily. She kept looking at the smudge of oil on the forehead, at the crown of the huge bald head glistening with water, and then at me—with such a smile. Like a beam from a lighthouse.

"Tsu-Mach. Tsu-Mach" It didn't sound anything like Thomas. She didn't care. Dragged him away from me and carted him off happy as sunshine with his useless legs swinging and slapping against her. Did she know what she'd done? For me, for the Church? For Thomas?

*Returned then to the Lady Margaret about eight and enjoyed a proper feast of beans & salt pork. The night being somewhat raw, I was persuaded to remain on board, Captain C. having already determined to weigh anchor and*

*continue his northward passage in the early morning. Said*
*Mass on deck in a grey dawn and bade Father Lawrence*
*farewell.*

I thought I had felt dispirited before. In those other
villages. But nothing compares with this. It's not loneliness—it's desolation. Yes, I am deserted. Utter, utter
desolation down there on the beach this morning,
watching the long boat row back after they put me
ashore, turning to stand in front of all those faces again.
A mountainous surge of loneliness. A tidal wave of it at
my back. Hopes, dreams, memories.

All I knew, all I valued, my prayers, my past, yes,
my Church. All these chattels I cart about with me
towering in a solid mass at my back and crashing down
around me where I stood on the stones. And all of
them useless here, sucked away in the receding wave,
leaving me, alone, on the shore.

*Then stepped ashore about seven with no other company to*
*single-handedly lay the foundations for the kingdom of God*
*here on this savage coast. May Jesus Christ be with me.*
*Amen.*

## POOR-BABY-THOMAS

there is water on my face    burning me like fire    it
runs in my eyes like tears    and the smoke of it is
sweet

## THE GIRL

Now the Old Woman became angry to see her only heir following the Priest, the childless father, like a sick dog, but nothing she could say could quite discourage the Girl. The Girl was waiting for the power of the White Shaman to take effect. She was patient, but still the man, her uncle, rolled to her in the night, and the head of the infant continued to grow. Nor had the young man, the Beautiful Boy, come to ask for her. The Girl began to lose hope.

One day in her despair the Girl took the infant boy to the edge of the waves where the shells chattered in the small surf. She took water and poured it on the baby's head as the Priest had done and she prayed. It seemed to her that if only she could make the baby's head stop its swelling then the Beautiful Boy would come to take her for a wife and then she would be delivered from the monstrous man. And as she poured the water she saw how it returned to itself in the waves and how every thing is one thing and it came to her that if only the monster that moved the man could be destroyed then the baby would be well and she would be married.

It was clear to her as the tide is clear after its turning: no one but the White Shaman, the childless priest who called himself Father, had the power that would destroy the monster. The Priest was like a tree that draws the lightning to itself. She would tell him all her pain.

That night, when the rain had driven the people early to sleep, she went to the Priest in the small hut the people had built for him and said, "Father-not-father, I have something to tell you."

But the Priest, when he had heard her story, went not to the Girl's uncle, the Old Woman's son-in-law, but to the Chief of all the People. And then all the village knew this thing and there was a purging and a cleansing such as the people had not seen in their lives before.

Always afterwards in the darkness the Girl would remember the man, her uncle, choking on a snore as the men woke him, the man kicking as they reached for his legs and bound him. In every darkness after that first she would see the man's tongue lolling like a dead dog's, see his eyes rolling and him dragged by the feet out of the house while the red wattles of his throat fell back over his nose and mouth and he stifled on his own flesh.

When they had killed the man they burned his house, and the man's body blistered and spat inside it. The Girl they took away past the sacred ridge of the Burial Ground and on up through the trees to where the snow creeps down in winter. There, where the river crashes over the cliff at the foot of the Holy Rock, there, beside a still, deep pool, they left her, stripped and painted with ochre, for the water to wash her and the wind to dry her.

For three days and three nights the Girl fasted and cleansed. Each night in her sleep she turned and saw again the man at her back, his bleared eyes housing the monster and his breath carrying the smell from the trading post.

On the fourth night she let herself become small like a pine needle, like a fish scale, so that when the terrible face appeared and breathed upon her she floated away and was carried on a wave into the throat of a white gull. The gull flew with her high into the empty sky.

A white gull screaming into the wind.

In the morning, she made her way back. When she came to the ridge where her ancestors rested in the trees above the village, she looked down and saw the smoke still hanging above the burned house, like a cloud, covering what had happened. The sun made planks of light through the smoke, down into the charred wood.

Then she walked to the house of the Priest and asked him to teach her how to pray to his Lord Above.

## THE PRIEST

It's been nearly two months and still no church. All the timber they hewed for me in those first weeks is lying out there, the cut surfaces flaring orange in the wet. They built my house quickly enough but once I was in it they seemed to lose all momentum. I've talked and reasoned with them as best I can but they don't seem to understand. One of them said the Lord Above will not be shut in a house. I did see his point. But that leaves us without a place to say Mass. The longhouse is out of the question. It's a heathen stronghold and there'll be no changing it, I can see that, for years to come. There's always God's fresh air but then there's always God's sweet rain too, and it's torrential here. An ark would be more in order.

*3RD JANUARY 1861   Work on the church has been hampered considerably not only by the inclement weather but also by the constant feasting & other pagan practices which bedevil the lives of these people. To name but one such, there was a heathen feast at the neighbouring village five miles to the north, at which excesses of every kind were encouraged.*

The very place that gave us the silent welcome last time, forlorn and dismal and the people not much better than savages. And Christmas Day, too. It was an insult to any social creature, let alone our good Lord. Such gluttony, such ludicrous displays of largess, for no better reason than to puff up the pride of the giver. But worst of all was some horrid ritual where men in masks ran on all fours with shreds of flesh dangling from their teeth. Unspeakable paganism. I should never have gone.

I celebrated, if that is the word, alone in the shelter of the deep eaves of the longhouse and thought of Christmas in the parish. There are times when I could wish myself back with all the busy, interfering bodies of Victoria, all their tedious, venial obsessions to boot. The things I am escaping. My place at the annual recital and tea. Eat, nod, approve, eat some more. My time consumed along with the mince-pies and the grog. But there I was with the rain coming down in front of me like a curtain and behind me, sounding through the wall, the thundering of the dances.

*The whole affair lasting three days with six more of trading and of bartering and any hopes of celebrating the Nativity laid to rest until next year. Progress has been further hindered by various unpropitious events, chief of these being the perpetration of a most heinous crime. The matter being brought expressly to my attention, I was compelled to intervene on behalf of the victim and report the crime to the Chief, whereupon the criminal was swiftly brought to justice.*

Rough justice. What they did to him doesn't bear thinking about but at least they were quick. And thorough. And right, after all, is right. He was a vile old sinner. And justice is justice, whichever way you look at it...

And yet what could I do? I was caught off guard

right from the start, as soon as she came to me. Standing in front of me, all alone.

"My uncle, he has touched me." That, that was too much to take. Pastor or no pastor, I don't want to know what they do in their filthy hovels at night. To hear it in confession, through the grille, with eyes downcast, that is one thing. But this, this urchin standing there with her long eyes staring and her hair all wet and bedraggled, her brown shins sticking out from under her cedar cape. No. Too much to take. But what *could* I do? Turn away from my duty? Say nothing? I would have had him sent to Victoria, charges of incest properly laid, a decent trial. But there wasn't time. There was nothing I could do to save the wretch. God rest his soul.

*A period of cleansing or purification of some kind now obtains during which the victim seems to be markedly maltreated while the rest of the villagers take yet another opportunity to let the tools lie idle.*

I saw what they did to her, taking her away, naked and painted like any savage. She's up there now somewhere in the high woods, in this cold. They would not let me past their burial ground. How long she'll stay there I've no idea. Is my patience being tested as well as everything else?

*6TH JANUARY   It seems that for my simple act of intervention in the above stated case I am to be rewarded with an elaborate feast in my honour. Yet more delays for our building.*

It's all the old woman's doing of course, whatever it is

she's up to. How she got it together in time is beyond
me. She has gifts in there piled up to the rafters. Skins,
blankets, trinkets, pans. Where she got it from I'll never
know but it's all to give away. And everyone—hoping
for a decent gift—treating her like royalty, which of
course is exactly what she wants. Yet just three days
ago there she was all rigged out like a scarecrow, red
and black rags flapping around her, her clothes all torn,
face all streaked, and the rest of them all but spitting on
her as she went by. (She had the child, too. Thomas.
She's up to something there as well. She had it dressed
up in feathers and shells and she was keening over it
one minute, and anointing it the next. Making it out to
be some kind of godling—the old pagan.) Now she's
playing the dowager. I shall never understand them.

But what I'd really like to know is where I come into
it all. She makes no bones about saying what she thinks
of me here, and yet it looks as if I'm to be guest of
honour at this affair. What am I to make of that? Am I
supposed to believe that it is an honour to her? Or to
me? I can't say I trust her too well. Or at all. When I
told her to stop wailing yesterday because it wouldn't
do a bit of good she gave me a look that made my hair
stand on end. If I didn't know better I could almost
start thinking of witchcraft. God forgive me.

## THE OLD WOMAN

The day begins black like the howl of a wolf.
Heart open. Spirit running red.
Heart a cave and spirit gone.

Eyes watch. Faces turn. Yes turn away from my
strength. It hurts. It will hurt you, Priest, watching
now as if you never see red and black, never see shame
and anger. Take my people. Watch to see me break.
Well don't watch too close because my power coming
for you. Drive you away. What you think you want,
white-face Priest? No family, no line here. No-place
Priest, you don't belong. Break up our kinship, lead us
from our guardians. Then what you going to do? Go
back in the tall ship to the stone village? Leave us broken, turned, in pieces? Like clam shells. Scattered.
Think my people going to flap and thrash like beached
fish when you gone? No. The Old Woman knows how
to keep her children. Keep them from the white-face
Priest. Show them who holds the power. I can keep the
Girl, too, and all my line to follow. I can give her the
Beautiful Boy—and then see if she needs you. And
you? I will give you—*give* you—Priest, a place of
honour among us. And all the world will see who it is
who gives and who takes. Then who will be beholden?
And who will hold the power?

# II

THE PRIEST

1 6TH FEBRUARY  *I attended two days ago the scene
of a tragic accident at which I was able to render some
assistance, two young boys being brought out of the icy
water more dead than alive and one of them responding to
the carbonate of ammonia which I was able to administer
with positive results.* And the whisky. My last bottle.
But God be praised for the good it did. The boy sitting up with a start, the green hue on him vanishing
like a receding tide. *The other, less fortunate, was buried
yesterday. While I have tried to moderate all inferences
concerning restoration to life, my intervention in the
tragedy may well have increased my standing & indirectly
contributed to the general improvement of the lives of the
people here for I was permitted to witness the so-called
burial. What I saw confirmed that a great deal of
superstition and very little respect attend the remains of the
deceased.*

They put them in the trees. The dead in ramshackle
boxes rattling among the dead boughs. I shall not forget it. We went up in the early morning to the ridge,
the drumming and the shouting sending crows
screaming from the trees. The sun had just broken
through so that the grey shapes of the coffins began to
loom out at us. Lodged precariously high in the trees,

some of them had slipped and rested at clumsy angles.
There were bones among the moss. They put the boy
rather low on one of the great hemlocks, his coffin perhaps too light to go higher where the winter gales
would send it down. As they hoisted it up, the toys
inside rattled. When it was in place, the prayers began,
the pagan prayers. The young men, who a moment
before had been shouting orders to each other, were all
at once grief-stricken and wept along with the women.
I walked to the edge of the ridge and tried to pray. The
village and the beach and the inlet lay under a thin mist,
rose-coloured in the dawn. As I stood there a wind
began to get up from the water, combing away the fog.
I could not pray for watching all the beauty. Behind me
the tall trees began to creak in the wind. And then the
men began to sing.

*I shall institute a decent Christian burial for all as soon as
I am able.*

## THE GIRL

Now, just as the Girl had wished and the Old Woman had planned, there came to the door of her house the Beautiful Boy. For three nights his parents came to ask for the Girl and he came, in the way of the people, wrapped in a blanket, his head covered, to sit outside the house alone. For three nights the mother and the father of the Beautiful Boy bartered for her and the Old Woman resisted, as she ought, while the Girl, as they argued, went to the wall and spied through the cracks, watching him there waiting. Ocean in my heart. For three nights his family come, asking for me, the Girl, begging. Then on the fourth night they come again and the Old Woman says Yes.

So the marriage was arranged and was as it should be with dancers and with drums, ankles feathering the flames, and old loving fingered out in corners, under blankets. But someone brought rum from the trading post to raddle the face, addle the brains. And then the voices were too loud and the laughter too high. There was loving with no love. There was anger. The Sullen Man, her brother-in law, fell asleep with his face in the dirt and the Chief of all the People lay snoring. Behind the blankets of the marriage room the Girl waited, but, outside, her Beautiful Boy sat grinning into his lap while his friends shouted at him and pulled up their loin cloths in front of his face. The Priest left long before. His teeth were clenched in rage.

## THE PRIEST

*20TH FEBRUARY   Yesterday the girl was "married." The "wedding," one of the worst spectacles of pagan excess I have witnessed, was conducted in the longhouse. Although I was deemed a guest of honour, decency forbad I should attend for long lest I seem to condone their practices by my presence. I saw enough, however, to determine that the establishment of Christian marriage in this community is a priority.*

*A further concern to me is the unprecedented appearance of the demon rum in the village. I shall take steps immediately to prohibit its consumption. (Everything I have ever heard about the natives in this respect appears to be true. There seems to exist a weakness inherent in their blood which makes them quite unable to withstand the temptations or the effects of liquor.)*

*Today as they rouse themselves after their debauch there appears to be some consternation among them. Someone is missing. If it is a drowning it will be God's judgement.*

The girl's brother-in-law, the Sullen Man, is out there now in a bitter wind, wandering aimlessly, lurching from side to side, sometimes turning up his face to the sleety rain and howling like a soul demented. Some of the more sober ones come up to him from time to time

but he pushes them away. Down at the beach there is a
small crowd scanning the water. Not another drowning, please God.

*The church is almost finished, indeed would be, were it not
for these interruptions.*
*21ST FEBRUARY   Events here at a sorry pass. There
has been a kidnapping. The men say that members of a
neighbouring tribe have carried off the bride's sister. The
husband of this woman is mad with grief and dangerous to
all who approach him. Our Chief, moreover, is quite
incapacitated with alcohol.*

And will stay that way no doubt until he drinks himself
out of it. Flagons of it he has. He sleeps on them—when
he's not drinking the stuff.

*For this reason I have been approached by some to
accompany the party that sets out tomorrow morning to
restore the girl's sister to her husband.*

The girl of course. She trusts me. Heaven help us all.
The others have been wary, treated me like a new trading item. They've tested me, fingered and felt me,
measured me with their eyes and finally, grudgingly,
accepted the offer. But the girl has trusted me since the
beginning. Not only that, but she expects something of
me. Quite unlike my complacent parishioners who,
while they could claim to "expect great things" of me
(as long as I fulfilled their expectations halfway up the
rain-sodden coast), were themselves happiest when
they could expect nothing. Nothing to derange their
comfortable spirits or their beribboned bonnets. They
expected nothing, hoped for nothing and, for all I
know, prayed for nothing. Unless it were to keep the

unlikely soul contained until the day that they should
die and it get clean away to its heavenly reward without bothering them further. The girl is what I came to
find. A soul on the outside. Asking, expecting. And
she trusts me. God help us all indeed.

## THE SISTER

Oh, keep your Beautiful Boy, sister. Keep my husband too for all I care. This. This is what I want, what I crept away for, treading the grey stones of the beach as if they were duck eggs. Following him down to the water, keeping low, under the tent of stars, sliding into his boat like thieves. This is what we pulled the boat through the darkness for, our hands in the icy water so there would be no sound of paddles. This is what I want. This lover, whose teeth shine at me in the darkness, who comes at me still grinning with hands as quick as fish, slippery, in and out of me, with bony hips that grind down on me, and the teeth that shine. That bite in the dark places. Keep your Beautiful Boy. I take this lover that crawls over, crawls under me, that takes me like a dog jumping a bitch. And fierce too. We shall be safe in his village. There he does what he wants and no Chief and no Grandmother and no Father-not-father to tell him what to do. Or not to do. If they come for me he will fight like a madman.

THE PRIEST

1 *5TH MARCH*   *It will scarcely be difficult for the*
 *reader to comprehend the reason for my protracted*
*silence when I say that*—that what? How did it come
about? I am here to preach the Word of the Lord.
Not to get myself tangled up in their squalid
affairs—*that I have sustained a serious gunshot wound in
my arm. (Thank God it is the left.) I believe I came
within an inch of my life. Praise God that He chose to
keep me safe to continue His work. Here follows an
account of the incident.*

 *On 22nd February, twenty-five of us, well-armed, set
out in three boats for the next village, where we had
intelligence that the bride's sister was being held against her
will. The day was fair & brisk with a strong tide running
and we reached the settlement in good time without tiring
our men.*

 *Upon arrival the appearance of the heavily shadowed
water in the deep bay was straight away familiar for the
village was the same that had conducted the heathen feast at
mid-winter, the same that had offered such a forlorn &
dismal aspect on my first setting foot on these shores. This
day, however, the entire village had come down upon the
foreshore to witness our coming. It was evident that they
were somehow forewarned of our approach.*

The husband of the kidnapped woman, when he saw his
wife, made to leap out of the boat, but several wise fellows
restrained him, and our Chief's brother (the Chief being
still incapacitated) went ashore unaccompanied to signify
that we harboured no evil intent. For several minutes he
conferred with the neighbouring Chief and obtained
permission for the rest of the party to disembark. During
all this time the woman from our village was clearly
visible, her abductor standing close by her and putting his
arm about her in an attitude of protection so that our
wronged husband was beside himself with anger and only
force kept him from them.

After further conference it became clear that there was to
be no persuading their headman to let the woman go, nor
even any chance of the woman herself wanting to leave. It
was decided to hold an impromptu court. For this, each of
the two contenders for the lady was put in the custody of
six strong men from the opposing tribe & everyone, each
one of us as well as the rest of the village, old women,
dogs, babies and all, entered the great house.

It was a tiresome proceeding and I felt that at any
moment the strains it imposed might lead to violence. The
two men stated their case at very great length and then
selected a spokesman each to restate it.

Throughout the trial I remained in ignorance of the
identity of the presiding judge until at the end of the last
speaker's oration all eyes turned to me.

It quickly dawned upon me that as a disinterested
observer and belonging to neither tribe I had been selected
to pass judgement on this difficult case, nor was I in any
position to refuse this dubious honour, there being enough
firearms & knives at large to start a modest war.

Here I must confess that I had not followed the
proceedings as attentively as I might. I had, however,
sufficiently caught the drift of each case to be able to

*roughly weigh its merits. On the one hand, our wronged husband rested his case on the fact of his "marriage" to the girl's sister. Now to this fact I attached only slight importance, their "marriage" being no kind of marriage at all in the eyes of the Church. It is true that these people use the institution much in the way that we Christians do, but they walk away from the contract freely when it so suits them; for this reason I regarded the marriage as they do, as a business contract to be honoured, incurring only the displeasure of friends & family, but no sin, if broken.*

*The kidnapper, on the other hand, had a far stronger case it seemed to me, and his evidence further eroded the position of the so-called husband for it appeared that the woman had been his concubine since a time preceding her union with the husband. Now this, it was obvious, served clearly to invalidate her "marriage."*

*In the absence of the true marriage ceremony, common law was the only valid rule and the woman was clearly the common-law wife of the man who now stood before me on his own ground. This was my judgement.*

And it pleased every soul under that roof except one. How much safer it would have been had I reversed that judgement and left them to fight it out among themselves.

*When it was over, their Chief invited us to stay and feast with him as a sign of friendship, but our disappointed plaintiff, now more sullen than ever, refused point blank and made such a stand that we quit the place immediately, leaving behind, I fear, not a little ill-will on this account.*

*As we were getting ourselves embarked, a messenger from the village ran down to me and handed me something wrapped in cedar bark, a gift of thanks, he said, from the woman.*

*We made our way back without any incident and, in contrast to the tension of the outgoing journey, in great good humour, I myself feeling not a little of the prevalent mood of relief at a crisis averted.*

*On our arrival we were greeted by a contingent anxious to hear the outcome of the mission.*

It was one thing to have passed judgement, quite another to account for it. The old woman was furious. She spat in my face. The girl was more accepting. She came to me later and apologized. I showed her the gift, a bracelet from her sister, and gave it to her. It wouldn't do to appear to have been bribed. And a gift from a woman like that...I asked the girl if she wouldn't let me marry her to the young man who has taken her for a wife. I made a lot of her sister's affair and tried to show her how her own marriage could never be in doubt—not if she had a proper Christian marriage. I think I can talk her round.

*After taking a simple meal with these people, I found myself overcome with fatigue from the journey & the excitement and so I retired early to bed—but not to rest. In the middle of the night I was woken by loud cries from a person outside approaching my house. Sensing danger I jumped from my bed, whereupon the door was flung open violently and there clearly outlined against the bright night outside was the sullen husband, musket in hand. I owe my life partly to the brightness of the moonlight outside—for the man looking into the darkness could not see, I think, as well as I inside the hut looking out—and partly to the friendship of the malformed cur that had taken to sleeping, against my will, underneath the bed.*

How many times had I kicked that dog out, poor beast? He was meant to save me. I was so tired that

night I forgot to look for him. At the sound of the door
he shot out from under the bed like a pea from a pod,
while I stood scared more than half to death without
even the presence of mind to grab my pistol from the
bedside.

*He, affrighted by the loud crack of the door thrown back on
its hinges, skittered out from beneath the bed & made for
the door, entangling himself beneath the feet of the intruder
and causing the man to fall as he was about to step into the
room. Whether or not he took aim I cannot say but there
was a loud report and a flash. For many moments I was
not aware that I had been shot but fell upon the intruder
and hollered with all my might, whereupon help arrived in
the shape of those who had been in pursuit trying to avert
the attack.*

All the moments that I lay there were like years. I shall
not forget them. Lying on the man in the dark, feeling
the heat of his body beneath me, smelling the grease on
his skin, the drink on his breath. He was winded, I
think, in the fall because his breath came rasping out of
him. It was the noise of an animal. And under my hand
I felt a stickiness oozing on his neck and it seemed to
me in that splinter of a second before I knew that the
blood was my own that God was immersing me in this
man's very body, that I was sent not to preach to these
people but to enter them, wholly.

*As soon as it was clear that the danger was over, my hurt
became apparent. The ball had passed right through my
arm and there was a great flow of blood. After that I
remember nothing more but awoke the next morning safe in
my bed attended by the old woman. She has cared for me
daily ever since and my wound is on the way to healing.
Praise be to God.*

The old woman. Of all people. I do remember. I
remember lying awake all night, half in, half out of
consciousness, sure that I was dying, not sure what to
do about it. I tried to pray but the words were con-
fused and the wrong names—the Spirit of the Mountain, the Mother of the Sea—slid in and out of my
prayers like ghosts. I began to be uncertain who I was,
what I was praying for. I knew only that I wanted to
live. So badly. Rejecting the call to God. When I saw
the woman by my bed it was as if some witchcraft had
been perpetrated. There was no longer any priest, nor
any pagan. There was only a son, in pain, and a mother
close by to soothe it. I was never further from Jesus. Or
closer?

*16TH MARCH   On my feet again today. Every day
seems to be an improvement on the last. I should be able to
resume my duties by the end of the week.*

Whatever the old woman did seems to have worked.
Though *why* she did it. . .? Some sense of honour? Or
guilt? The more I think about it, the more I feel the
whole incident had a purpose, was sent, in a strange
way, for my own good, the good of the mission. I
know one thing: I could have the support of all the
Bishops in the world, the agreement of all the chiefs,
but I wouldn't have a hope here without *her* approval.
Truly God moves in mysterious ways. Perhaps next
time He won't take me quite so much by surprise.

*There is talk now of the punishment due to my assailant.
These people have a strong sense of justice and of honour.
I, however, feel little inclined to provoke this man further.
17TH MARCH   Have decided today to send a messenger
to Victoria with an account of the incident.*

*But I almost forget the most momentous entry I have yet
to make in this journal. Our church is complete. Thanks
be to God. The natives here—in an effort, I wonder, to
appease me & make amends—laboured most diligently
during my indisposition and completed the building. We
celebrate Mass under a Christian roof tomorrow.*

# III

## THE GIRL

Now the Girl lived peacefully with her husband, the Beautiful Boy, and her brother the Poor-Baby-Thomas. The Beautiful Boy was young and loved his friends but still he was kind to her and every day brought her new gifts. At night when they went together to the far corner of the Old Woman's house where they slept apart from all the others she would love to lie and look at him, his skin shining like copper and his lashes lying like feathers on his cheeks. It was all her pleasure. But when he rolled to her in the dark and covered her, the blanket like wings over the water, she was afraid to hear again her uncle's voice and so would only close her eyes and bear it and wait for him to finish. Afterwards, when he went to sleep, she would gently roll his weight from her shoulder, her thigh, slide over to the child and hold him for comfort until her limbs had stopped their shaking. But she did not stop loving the Beautiful Boy. When daylight came and he went out to hunt or fish, she would take up the child again and carry him with her to dig for the wild camas or to look for the strong salt grass for her baskets.

Sometimes she would go to the house of the Father-not-father. He had cloth to give her and fine needles and she sat on the floor of his house and sewed for the child a suit of clothes in blue cloth with trousers like the sailors' and a long robe like the Priest's.

Then she would be almost happy, feeding the child and caring for him, then sewing again while the Priest talked to her and taught her new worlds of magic and of prayer.

But still the Girl longed to see her brother well. She begged the Priest to help her.

THE PRIEST

*2*7TH MARCH   *A glorious day in the unfolding*
*history of our church. A cross hewn of yellow cedar was*
*erected today on the foreshore. A true sign of welcome to*
*all who venture here.*

The way of the cross. And how many stations to make
along the way. But it's done. Despite all the objections
and protestations, despite the elders and the women
and the conniving mischief-makers who just like to
make things difficult, it's done. And I thank God. Not
that anyone will ever see it. That is not important. I
need it for myself, for me. It is a marker, *my* mark. It
says that I am here. Sometimes I feel as if I shall dissolve
in the incessant mist, as if I were not really here at all.
  The mist, the interminable rain.
  Here everything drips, dissolves, melts into the grey
damp. Here even the surfaces of the rocks shiver with
the water that glistens over them. Nothing is stable.
Everything regresses. There is a morbidity about this
land that is inescapable. Here the whole of nature bends
to decay. The trees are hung and draped with green-
grey lichen in shreds. Shrouds. They loom in the mist.
The very houseposts rot where they stand. And the
yellow cross?

But we do move forward. We do. There has been progress. We have the church. And that is everything.

*31ST MARCH   A fine spring day. I took this opportunity for a solitary walk in the surrounding woodlands to refresh my eyes and my spirit with new perspectives. The land here, so awesome and horrid in foul weather, is endowed with a natural beauty in fine.*

I had climbed to the burial ground before I knew it. The quiet. I thought I could just make out voices from the village. It could have been bird calls.

The burial ground looked not so appalling in the sun. All the white lilies under the trees, the sun splashing through onto the clearing in front of them. The weathered wood of the boxes shining silver where the sunlight struck them. Dried out, light and brittle. Like the bones inside. The new ferns in the shadows down below. All the new life springing.

*I walked as far as the burial ground where I considered how best to reform the customs in present use.*
*11TH APRIL   Have received word today that a contingent from Nanaimo will be passing through and will escort my assailant to Victoria for trial.*

*On the subject of discipline, I have found it necessary to institute a set of rules governing dress & behaviour at Mass. Education in certain matters is a priority. I may be able to use the most responsive members of the community to this end, especially the young girl who was of so much use in the early days.*

She's here almost every day, trailing in with the child in tow. So big now she can't carry him, but has a cedar board attached to strings and must drag him along, like a fat seal. They seem happy enough, both of them. She brings her work to do. Plumps the child down in a corner and he drools and sucks his fingers while she weaves with grass, or sews. Sometimes she'll listen to me. Her faith is a gift. She doesn't say too much but today she asked me if I would cure the child. And she believed, really believed I could. Her expression was as flat as the cedar board when I said I couldn't.

"Oh, yes you can," she said. Just like that. Straight. Toneless. And she wouldn't go away. Sat right down in the middle of my cabin and said, "I can wait."

I told her I couldn't heal him, but I could treat his soul. I said I would administer the sacrament of the sick. On one condition: you marry your Beautiful Boy—*my way*.

She didn't even blink. "When?" she said.

Bartering with the sacraments. God help me if I've done wrong. I've tried to explain, to tell her it's not in my power. But she's still expecting a miracle. She believes in me—but she doesn't believe me.

*She of course will be married decently by me as soon as she and her bridegroom have received a fitting course of instruction.*
*9TH JUNE   Accompanied a small party to the trading post fifty miles north.*

It was a good trip. Less than a year I've been here, but it might as well be six. I'm so close to these people now that sometimes I can't see what is happening in front of my face. When they show me how to smooth a board or repair a trap I think I'm learning more from them than they are from me. And sometimes when I sit with them and dip my fingers in the dish of grease and sip the sour berry mash I am not sure who is changing, who is being changed.

Times there are when I feel so far away from home.

What does it matter if they hear my word? Or don't hear it? And besides, do I ever really know who hears, who doesn't? They go on with their rituals just the same, mumbling their spells. They have a heathen prayer for every little thing they do. They're never going to change their ways. There are souls at home who are ready, who've been listening all their lives, only waiting for another word, to push them over into salvation. I should be saving those, the ones who have a chance.

And then one of the heathens smiles at me, offers me a basket of sweet shoots, tells me some special story. And I know that he must have a chance, too. However slight.

Then again I look at the church. Church! A shed, a shack, cobbled together. And I think, this is no progress at all, this is a sacrilege against the Lord. And I hear the people gabbling the responses without meaning, nor wanting any, and I think this is a mockery, this is blasphemy. They are no better than the idiot baby.

One has to step away from these fears and these doubts. The trip gave me time. Step after step with nothing to think about but getting there. When we stopped in the deep woods I heard again the voice that calls me, keeps me here. And I prayed for light in the darkness.

*We set out just before dawn two days ago and reached Fort Jamieson at about five in the afternoon. We made a quick meal and having skins to sell set to business immediately.*

*At the conclusion of the transaction Mr. Skully entertained us with his lively stories. In the course of the evening I learned the fate of the girl's brother-in-law who, after a fair trial in Victoria, was sentenced to twenty years imprisonment.*

*We rested that night with Mr. Skully and the next day*
*refreshed our spirits according to our tastes, I in savouring*
*the pleasures of new surroundings, and the natives in*
*visiting a nearby camp.*

Twenty years. I had to step outside when he told us.
Twenty years. There was no air in the smoky room. I
could have gagged on the stench of the tobacco I had
been smoking, the whisky I had drunk, the rancid fat,
the sweat, the smell of the malt. Outside I could smell
the stable—and it was preferable. I walked on. Great
waves of cool air came splashing through the dark
branches, the sweet cedar.

Twenty years.

Next morning I walked out again. Fort Jamieson is
lodged in a crab's claw of land and I walked to the tip
of the northern pincer. There an island rears out of the
sea. An immovable object, steep and solid, ponderous.
Unalterably grave. As his sentence is to him.

The smaller islands lay all around, a chain of them,
blue and green, dwindling south to the horizon, man-
oeuvring in the mists to the north, stealing by the great
mountains. I had to close my eyes.

*We made our way back today, the canoes loaded with fresh*
*provisions of flour & rice & molasses, a peck or two of*
*beans, some salt pork and a little baked bread. We*
*purchased too some nails and some tin, one or two axe*
*heads & a good length of chain.*

Twenty years.

*12TH JUNE   Nine months since my arrival on these*
*shores, and a fitting time to take stock. The shooting*
*incident of last March has had a strangely tonic effect on*

*relations between us. The old woman has become a true
friend to me and there are few if any dissenters. There is
great opportunity here for a Christian community to
flourish now that it has taken root.*

*Sunday Mass is well established and attendance is
usually fair since fishing at that time has been discouraged;
one or two of the congregation manage a reasonable attempt
at the responses; some are keen to sing; public decency has
been improved by a mutually agreed law requiring trousers
to be worn by men in attendance at Mass or at my house;
we have established our own police patrol to enforce these
laws & others pertaining to peaceful conduct; new souls
that enter this life are duly baptized and those departing are
given a decent burial which though it may not be in
consecrated ground does at least evince a suitable degree of
respect for the remains.*

*Progress has indeed been great. We hope soon to ensure
that all young people will partake of the sacrament of
matrimony. If the girl's wedding goes well.* She, as useful as ever, knows some of the Gospel now, says she
will teach the children. There's so much that can be
done. A little more industry, a little more ambition.
That's all it would take. And time. They've swallowed
so many changes already. Or are they just waiting for
the chance to spit? We shall see.

*30TH AUGUST   Our first Christian wedding today.
The church decorated with cedar boughs and mats for the
occasion and all the village in attendance.*

All those people, all that crowd, and yet, waiting there
out of the bright sun, I had the same feeling that came
over me when I first arrived, standing alone on the
beach. I stood before them, my flock, and they before
me, and there was a wilderness between us—and yet
they did not see it. They looked straight across at me,

into my eyes. They trust me. They believe I am on firm ground and they trust me to reach out and bring them safe across. And oh, God. I feel so alone to do it. Help me, my God. *In thee, O God, I put my trust.* Help me my God because alone I am not sufficient.

*The bride was decked in an ancient cedar costume. Readers at home will be greatly entertained to hear that the groom came with his face painted. The young couple, duly prepared by me over the last several weeks, were well versed in the responses and maintained a dignified and thoughtful composure throughout. I could not help thinking that a fine precedent has been set for the proper establishment of matrimony in our community.*

## THE OLD WOMAN

Something happening here and who to stop it? Nothing will stop it. Something rolling towards us over us. A wave. My song the salmon impaled. I bleed. People in the church clams in a basket. Tongueless. See all the village gathered at the word of the wifeless Priest for this wedding of his. See them all gathered silent. All. Mouths open spirits gone. No singing no dancing. No stories. Wifeless Priest use my Girl use her Beautiful Boy like the Storyteller use his dancing figures. But no dancing. Look at the wooden wife the wooden husband. Mouths holes in the masks of shamans. Mouths open mouths close. Words fall out. Something happening. And I powerless. Empty and hollow. It is the Priest. No songs no prayers no laws shrink his power. He grow tall among us like a figure in the body of a tree. Make the People forget their work make them forget old ways forget old duties and the dues they owe the spirits. Forget the spirits. The most holy places in our lives he denies.

Listen. There was a burial. Wife of the Chief die and a box made. No more corpses in the trees, the Priest say. Earth is the holy place, say the Priest. Slaves then scrabble in the ground like dogs. A hole made and she put in covered up with dirt like dung while the wailing

of her sisters clings to the trees. But she will not stay
and that same night she herself scrabble at the ground
from under. Heave herself up and her hand all blood-
ied lie on the open black earth like a fungus. Priest say
box not strong hole not deep and dogs the living dogs
did smell her out and pull her from the grave. Who
believe the Priest?

And again a birth. Listen. No more dancing woman,
the Priest say. Priest send her away she all decked in her
red and her feathers he send her away from the house of
labour. So the mother a young girl squat all night
sweating bleeding and the baby born with the cord
around his neck and no dancing woman to hurl life into
him and he die. Priest say the baby dead inside the
mother. Who believe the Priest?

Now here my Girl a second time marry her Beautiful
Boy and the Priest say no man can set them apart.

## THE GIRL

After the Father-not-father had married her to her Beautiful Boy inside the church, the Girl hoped for even greater happiness. When the ceremony was over she left her husband's side and went straight to the idiot child, her brother, and dragged him to the Priest. Now, she said, you must keep your promise. The Priest sighed but he laid the child on the ground outside his house and opened his Book of Words again. Then he prayed to his Lord Above and at the same time drew signs with his magic oil on the child's great head and on his hands and feet. And all the time the Poor-Baby-Thomas stared and drooled and whimpered in a small voice. When he had finished, the Girl picked up her brother, wrapped him in fur and laid him down to sleep in the house where she dwelt with the Beautiful Boy. That night when she lay in the arms of her husband her thoughts were all with Poor-Baby-Thomas. In the morning she woke early and straight away rolled over to the child. The fur was cold. At first she thought the child was cured for he was not there, and she ran outside calling for him. Her husband woke and the others too and they stood at the door of the house. Then the Beautiful Boy went inside and returned with the fur. He strode down to the poles on the beach and stood, shaking the fur and shouting: Where is the Poor-Baby now, Priest? Tell me where is the Poor-Baby now.

A great crowd gathered and from that day there were many who suspected the Priest of great evil.

## POOR-BABY-THOMAS

the smoke of the fire burns my eyes     my tears are
flames     the girl     the girl     i want her to hold
me     she is not here     the moon is here     only
the moonface big and round and shining like
copper     it flies behind the high smoke     it shakes
like water and vanishes     the smoke fills my eyes fills
all the sky     the moonface comes again trembling wet
out of the smoke     it bends nearer to me nearer     it
is not the moon not the girl     it is a beautiful
face     it is beautiful     i love this face trembling near
to me     it makes me smile     its breath smokes
sweet over my face and its hands slip up from the
darkness to cover my eyes from the smoke to cover my
mouth     the beautiful face is very close     i feel it
near in the blind dark     it is going to breathe the
moon into me     the moon will fill me will fill me

# IV

## THE SISTER

I saw them all today out at the ship. Everyone for miles around out on the water to be first on board, to strike the best bargain. Sister was there, fat with a baby. Grandmother. The Priest of course, already on the ship. Lording it, as he always did. It pleases me to know I am not one of them.

We spoke, Sister and I, and she told me how it is with the Priest and his new laws. To do this, to not do that. Let him try to tell us what to do. She says he's going to the place where they hold my husband prisoner. Let him not interfere. I am happy with my lover, who loves me still, better than any husband.

She said she is happy with her Beautiful Boy, so happy she has married him twice. I laughed and patted her belly.

"No, this," she said, "this is the spirit of our Poor-Baby-Thomas"—and she believed it. Then I laughed until I choked. She told me how the Priest had laid his hands on the Poor-Baby and set his spirit free.

"Did you see it go?" I asked. "Can you tell me where it is now?"

"No," she said. "In the morning I woke up and he was gone. Free."

Can she believe that? Not in her belly. I am not a

child. Or a fool. There is something bad there. I asked
Grandmother. She only smiled.

"What is it to you?" she said. "You are not one of
us." I waited. "Everyone believes what he wants," she
said.

"And you, Grandmother? What do you believe? Did
the Priest kill him?" But she would only smile.

"All I know," she said, "is that there are some who
believe it."

## THE PRIEST

*20TH APRIL 1862   The Venture, a trading vessel out of Vancouver, anchored yesterday in the bay. There was much activity all day in the trading of skins for molasses* which should improve the cooking considerably *and arms* as if they don't have enough *and trinkets. I have spent all day in the company of Captain Vandyke, dined with him and will spend the night on board, having determined to sail with them tomorrow to Victoria.*

Do I have to justify it? I did not intend to go, did not plan it this way, but the company is fresh—and at least we understand each other. Besides, the food, coarse as it is, is an enticement I'm ready for. Lawrence wouldn't turn down such an opportunity. And I'm not leaving them for good. I've worked hard enough, God knows. There has to be something to lift the spirits. Day after day all through the winter, sleety rain and bitter winds and hardly the sight of another face, everyone hidden under capes and blankets, nothing to do but chop wood to keep warm and sit by the fire to get dry. The snow at midwinter a gift from God for its brightness alone but muddied and fouled in no time only to freeze again solid into glassy lumps along with the rigid mud.

Then day after day of bone-aching cold with not even blue sky overhead but a layer of dirty cloud like frozen fog.

And the people as unyielding. All winter they went about their business as if I'd never set foot on their shore, turning up at Mass all right, but with about as much sense of devotion as any well-upholstered nabob in a fancy waistcoat. They haven't given up their feasts. Coming to Mass has been a way of passing the time, keeping warm, the way I chop wood with the wood pile full.

And yet last summer I could hope. Everything was in my favour—until the child, the idiot baby. All my hopes vanished along with him. Nothing has been the same since. Suspicion and mistrust left behind like traces after the kill. *Was* he killed? They never found the body. But that he should disappear on the very night that I administered the sacrament of the sick...? So that all eyes rested on me? There's something strange about the whole affair: the girl's acceptance, her husband's rage, his haranguing the seagulls on the wind that day down on the beach. The old woman's silence. If someone killed the child—and how else could it disappear—and then wanted to incriminate me, why wouldn't he leave the body as evidence? Why leave this empty space where each one comes and lays down his suspicion like an offering? Fear? Someone afraid of his own crime? Afraid of his victim? Or afraid of me? Someone who thought I might have power enough to restore life, make of an infant's corpse a living indictment?

But without the corpse there is only doubt all round. Some of them, the girl for one, say they don't even believe the child is dead. Whoever was trying to discredit me has done just the opposite as far as she's concerned. All that day sitting quietly while the search was on. She'd taken his fur from her husband, folded it over and sat with it in her lap, stroking it.

"He's free," she said. And I could have agreed but she had to go on, "You've released his spirit. He's free now to find a new body."

Utter faith. Only it's not what I wanted her to believe. But there was no convincing her otherwise.

Faith divorced from fact. How many times have I preached it at home, argued it with non-believers who wanted the hard evidence, who would not, could not believe without indisputable, incontrovertible facts laid out like exhibits on a courtroom desk? Belief is not contingent on proof. Belief and proof, I used to tell them, may never be related, they belong to separate worlds. Now I know.

*There I shall attend the Bishop who seems to have conveniently forgotten my existence & investigate the circumstances of the brother-in law, who has been much on my mind of late (it being a year since he was imprisoned) besides which, this taste of civilization gives me an appetite for a thorough repast.*

## THE GIRL

Now the Girl gave birth to a child who came from the darkness where Poor-Baby-Thomas had gone. In her heart she thanked the Priest for the magic he had made. Watching the child, her daughter, suffocate at her breast, she could almost be happy. She could forget the trouble she had known and the pain that she had received and she could almost forget the words she heard on the night of the birth as she knelt on the floor of the house, he, her Beautiful Boy, kneeling beside her, his lips on her ear. "Listen. I have to tell you. I have to tell you." Then her own voice, "No. I will not hear it. No!"—her screaming tore his voice in shreds and brought the Old Woman shambling and shaking and calling for the midwives. The women, happy, took her away to the hut that was prepared for her, placed her on the birth mat and circled her round with prayers and with songs. Outside, despite the Priest and all his laws, the dancing woman danced, while, inside, the child in the Girl thundered to get out and in great shaking waves was born.

Then in came the Beautiful Boy magnificent in a cloak of feathers. He stood before her and spread the cloak wide. And a mask covered his mouth.

The Girl cried, though her tears were neither for the pain nor the joy.

## THE SISTER'S HUSBAND

One whole turning of the year. That is what he tells
me. But there is no need to tell. Though I am kept
like a mink in a cage, I know. There is a window barred
with iron as thick as my thumb. It shows me day and
night, nothing more. But I know. The window tells
nothing. It is an adze chip of sky, blind. I am locked
away from the green fern uncurling, the seal pups peb-
bling the water, but I know. I knew when the berry was
ripening on the bush, when the wolf was creeping hun-
gry to the meat under the roof. The light crept with
each day's dawn further round the wall, from the iron
bucket on one side to the end of the cot—and back
again. It is one whole turning. I sleep and I wake.
Sometimes I wake to a pink light and night follows
without a day. Sometimes I sleep through nights and
days together. I sleep because I am cold. Here I have
been cold all my life. Wrapped in blankets I am already
dead. When I get up from the floor my legs are frozen,
will not unbend. The Priest has locked up my blood.
He has taken everything from me. He took my wife,
my freedom, now he takes my life's blood. He has
taken away everything that was mine—the taste of the
clam, the rain on the salal. Here there are only walls that
sweat and faces that shout and food that smells rotten.

He says he will take me back though the men here say his mercy is too good for me. Does he think I will go back like a slave, a captured beast licking his heels?

## THE PRIEST

*21ST MAY   Made up the coast on a heavy sea, news of our coming everywhere preceding us so that we were greeted at each stage by a veritable flotilla of small craft. The poor weather in no way deters the Indians who are eager to do business with the captain and bring him a fair amount of trade. We expect to make the mission before noon tomorrow.*

"Home." More like home than Victoria—however much I looked forward to being there, leading a civilized life for awhile, treating with my own countrymen, enjoying all the refinements I have turned my back on. Mass in the cathedral, luncheon with the Bishop, meetings of the Diocesan Committee, special receptions, dinners, the jellied veal we all know is pork, the good brandy if you happen to be in favour. It was all a performance I had seen before. Only this time I was an actor caught speechless when the curtains opened.

What could I possibly have to say to them, the nodding, eager ladies at the mission dinner? Would they like to know the attendance at Mass, the progress of the Sunday school? No, they had other lines of enquiry.

"I suppose they must be tremendously savage?" Mrs.

Hildstrom earnest, hopeful, turning up her face for her bonnet to funnel the upsetting truth, not to miss a drop. "And the dreadful rumours are true, you found?" Miss Beechley, too nice to specify but craving all the same, sawing at her cold pork as if to demonstrate the unspeakable, the consumption of human flesh.

"But your arm, Father." Everyone tasting the thought. "You must live in fear of your life."

So I told them what they really wanted to hear: how the men dress like wolves for the dance, how the women paint themselves for a birth. I could have just tossed them a few words—"blood" "feathers" "nakedness"—and they might have drooled, happy.

But I got my money.

And the new lumber, planed and true to build the schoolhouse, and all the hardware to furnish it. Not forgetting the two dozen curtain rings. For the fingers of two dozen Christian brides.

And a promise from the Bishop to come to us. He puts it off.

I asked Lawrence if he'd like to get leave to come up with me.

"Not this time," he said. "I'm getting past it." He looked hale enough to me, had eaten enough for four men at dinner and sat up drinking half the night, demolishing the characters of most of his parishioners and putting away a vast breakfast before seven thirty the next morning.

"Well you don't look as if you've deteriorated too much since I last saw you."

"Ah, it's not my style," he said. "I leave it to you younger men."

I should have liked someone to talk to, but how could I sit in his study with his prints of Irish foxhounds on the walls and his shelves full of rare tobaccos and talk about the old woman and what a mystery she is to me, about the girl and how I pray for her? Such a capacity to love. And then the plight of this poor fellow in the hold—broken now, I could tell as soon as I saw him in his cell, and with no spirit, it seems, to mend.

The ship rolls badly. I pray God the poor wretch is a good sailor. He shouldn't be in the hold. But nothing I could say would induce him to stay with me. The sailors would have put him on the deck.

"I am no man's dog," he said. With a scowl on him like a cur's.

## THE SISTER'S HUSBAND

The boat creaked. It creaked all night with the sound of the high trees. The place where I lay was big and dark. There was green slime between the boards. Great boxes tied with thick ropes loomed, groaning. It smelled of hemp and iron, raw wood and a sharp smell like pine burning. It smelled too of mould and molasses and bad water. I found a corner small and tight away from the boxes and stayed there. Creaking. Rocking. Once I woke and the darkness was like winter. A storm from the sea was making the high trees sway and I in my burial box had my knees drawn up to my chin, the sides of the box too close for me to move, the box itself wedged tight in the branches but the branches rocking, rocking. I could hear the voices of the dead as they groaned in their trees. I did not sleep after that.

The Priest would have had me beside him. In his power. The sailors would have had me on the deck with the hens and the great horned animal that bellows in its cage of wood. But I have come back a free man. And not beholden.

When the sickness passes and I am strong enough to walk abroad, I shall go first across the water and bring back my wife. The Beautiful Boy has said he will help

me but I shall go alone without even my friends, who
though they smile now will desert me again at a word
from the Priest as they did when he passed his false
judgement. And I a fool ever to believe the Priest had
power to judge, to decree. No man has the power to
tell me my wife is not my wife—least of all a white-face
Priest, a Father-not-father without a woman of his
own. I shall go alone and at night. I need no one to help
me. I shall slit the throat of the man who stole my wife
and I shall bring her back. And if the Priest is killed in
the war that will surely follow...

## THE PRIEST

2*2ND MAY Arrived in the A.M. on a fair sea, the wind having dropped considerably. We stood off in the bay and were soon surrounded by a great many canoes. About midday I went ashore in the tender with my charge. There was a decent welcome prepared for us but the brother-in-law remained surly throughout. We despatched canoes to unload our machinery and provisions, and bade farewell to the captain, who remained the rest of the afternoon at anchor conducting a brisk trade with the Indians.*

And, yes, it was a homecoming of sorts. This is my home. I could not leave these people. Now that I have them. The Chief hugged me like a brother. He may not be a strong man, or a great one, but he is kindly, tries to do the right thing.

Even the old woman smiled. She grinned, turned the girl round to show me the baby strapped on her back, a little black-haired mite, a girl. They like girls, seem to think them special, in some perverse way.

The girl herself seems changed.

*In the evening a feast at the great house. The brother-in-law not in attendance, which somewhat perturbed me. On*

*making investigation, however, when it was time to retire,*
*I found him in his bed, still sick from the rough passage.*

I hid the pistol I carried. There was no need for it. He
was lying there in the dark, staring. His mouth half
open as if in nausea. "You are not at the feast," I said.
And he turned his face to me. Eyes like a dead animal's. No malice, no resentment, only a blank stare as if
he didn't know me.

"Your people welcome you back to your home," I
said. "They are dancing for you in the longhouse."

He coughed harshly. "I am sick," he said and turned
to the wall.

To my relief. *I am sick.* Better than finding him
behind my door with a knife in his hand. God shield
me.

*25TH MAY   Began work on the new school house*
*today. The men, most of them, have set to with a will, the*
*fishing being slow at the present time and there being,*
*moreover, the attraction of the milled lumber and the new*
*tools. Some of the men still labour under the*
*misapprehension that they build a community house for*
*their feasting and their dances. They seem unable to*
*comprehend the idea of a place dedicated to learning. One*
*of them, the Chief's brother, returned lately from the*
*trading post, brings me news that the city of Victoria is in*
*the grip of an outbreak of smallpox. How old or how*
*recent this news I have no way of knowing. I thank God*
*we left when we did.*
*26TH MAY   The work goes on with progress more rapid*
*than in the building of the church and no abatement in*
*enthusiasm. At this rate we shall be finished within the*
*month & I shall be able to begin the training of the*
*catechumens as well as the full education of the children.*

This is God's work. Not committees and collections. Not parish teas and the notes for the next sermon. It is the hands of men labouring together. The sound of a hammer in the wilderness. We shall dedicate the school to Our Lady, Star of the Sea. We shall flood the young minds with light.

The girl will help me. I've heard her singing hymns to the baby. She has a good memory and she learns so quickly she'll be invaluable. If the old woman would stay out of the way, the dragon. Everything is fine —"Ah, Father-not-father, peace to you! The day is a good one"—until she thinks I'm on her territory, then she's unspeakable. Quarreling right now about the newborn. But the child is mine. God's anyway. The first child born to a Christian couple after a Christian marriage. I could have brought it into the world myself. It shall not be a heathen though the old woman is doing her best to make it one, insisting that the girl take it up to the burial ground for some godforsaken rite. But the girl—God bless her—won't go. She wants the child baptized.

## THE GIRL

The Girl loved her daughter dearly, called her her bird, her swallow and gave her her soul. She forgot her beautiful husband, forgot the Old Woman, the elders and the white-faced Priest, though she would sing their songs to the newborn. When she sang the words were not important. She laid her soul on the face of the sky, the clear face of evening and her swallow swooped there, played there, where the blue leached away to white, was endless. A not yet night.

> *Little bird full of grace*
> *The Lord is with thee*
> *Blessed art thou among the flocks of the sky*

The Priest said she must sing only the words he had taught her but the smallness of the child's fingers and the blackness of its eyes were enough to make words spring into her mouth. So she would go far away from the others and sing to the child where no one could hear. It was good besides to keep the child from the quarrelsome voices for the Old Woman would have her take it to the Burial Ground to be dedicated to her ancestors but the Girl would not agree. Her daughter's spirit belonged to Poor-Baby-Thomas and Poor-Baby Thomas did not dwell in the Burial Ground. The Girl decided to take her daughter instead to the Priest, though she did not tell him the name that she called her—Swallow-that-dives-in-the-heart—but kept it secret. The Priest named the child Mary.

## THE SISTER

The taste of his lips is still on mine. Though I've scraped and scraped and buried my face in the salt sea. The taste of him. The taste of the sickness. He said he was dying, said to Grandmother he would curse me if I didn't go to him. So I went. Her old hand a claw on my arm. Her feet shuffling over all the stones in the world and not making a sound, not a grate nor a click of pebble, silent down to the boat. Then over the dark water stealthily, like the time before. Slipping over the blackness. Into blackness. But this time Grandmother in the boat. Bent like a heron, paddling as if she would stab the ocean, would kill it. Grandmother dragging the boat onto the beach. Grandmother, the Old Woman leading me. The Old Woman, the Old Woman. Opening the door of the hut and pushing me in. And he was there. I could smell him. The foulness. He reached out with his blistered hand, pulled me down until his eyes stared into mine, waiting to curse me. So I closed my eyes to the blackened skin and lay my cheek on his burning, stinking mouth and he turned my face and held it in both hands and he kissed me.

The Old Woman is evil. I have come here once in secret, stealthily across the sliding waters and I can do it again. Only next time the Old Woman will not know that I come.

# THE BEAUTIFUL BOY

And yet when it began it had all been so fine. So fine. All the village gathered for me and my young wife. Honouring us a second time with their gifts: blankets of softest down, boxes of most excellent carving, knives and needles. All finery. All riches. The magic words of the Priest tumbling in the dark church. The magic rings upon our fingers. She said I was her painted man, her crested bird. Her kingfisher. And then, when the Priest at last had gone, her body again. Softly smoothly warm. A lake of clear water. Opening. And I, the kingfisher flashing fire, plunging into dark. Into no more sound of breathing.

The rest—the thing that I did afterwards in the darkness while she slept—the rest is like a dream remembered. But what I did to the idiot boy was not the end of it. It clung to me like a nightmare, like a drowning man with a hold on my neck. I wanted to shake free. I wanted to tell her. And could not.

The dream returned then each night after that. There was no other dream but this one, not a movement from his hands, nor a sound from his throat forgotten, everything there happening again as it happened that night, and his eyes, his idiot eyes looking into mine before they closed. Each night the dream lasted longer than the night before. Each day ended the sooner for the dream to begin.

And then one night it woke me. From inside her new swollen belly it woke me with a life of its own. I was asleep with no dream at all and in my back came a nudging, impatient, waking me, a leg twitching like a dog's in sleep. I turned and lay beside it, the stretched the terrible belly. Big like bladder with what was inside. Swollen like the head of the baby, the Poor-Baby-Thomas.

It froze the breath in my throat. I could not breathe with fear. What if it should speak from inside her? What if it should speak with the bubbling voice of the idiot boy? What if a face should form on the tight skin? What if I should stare at the veined tautness of the belly and an instability begin and the skin there make tracks and ripples and form into the pattern of a face, pressing up from inside? Trying to call my name, to tell the world what I had done?

And I could not enter her again. Could scarcely lie beside her.

Until at last I had to put his fretful soul to rest. Not under the ground where I had put him, in fear, with no ceremony, shovelling sand over his face as if he were no better than a dead dog, shamefully, like the people of the Priest. But with honour, in the way of the People, in the Burial Ground. I waited until the snooping Priest had one day gone away and I returned that night to the shameful ditch that I had made, dug up the withered body with its lingering stench and carried it away in secret to lay it in the holy place and honour it as it should be honoured, with songs and with dances, praying to the Spirit all the time not to strike me down but to see that I was a man of honour, a man who could swallow his fear and risk his life for the spirit of a child.

Only when it was time for the child, my daughter, to come to us did it seem as if the Spirit had not heard and was troubled still. Then I knew I had to tell or I would break apart. I held her by the shoulders, even while the child inside was shaking her, I held her, tried to tell her that it could be a monster, an idiot child come back to haunt us. I tried to tell her but the Girl, my wife, would not listen, heard only the new child, calling from the darkness like a bird.

So I waited. Outside, in my paint and my cloak, fine before the dancing woman. At last I heard the cry, shoved aside the flapping protests of the midwives and saw her there my daughter, perfect. Whole.

All so fine.

And now I am punished for the crime of silence, for the secret I have kept and for the gift that I have received, in guilt, and not told. I am punished by the Spirit who shows the world I am unworthy, unclean. And I must lie here while my fingers on my face crawl like crippled bugs over hot coals and my wife with my daughter watches from a distance, the Priest between us. My skin is blistered with the punishment and my lips are crusted like the mouth of the salmon over the fire.

But worse, there are others. I hear them in their distress. We are so few now that we cannot circle the fire at night.

Are all the People punished on my account?

## THE GIRL

It seemed to the Girl, when the sickness came upon her people, as if she had known all her life that happiness would never let itself be taken like a fish in a trap. Her Beautiful Boy fell to the sickness. They took him away from her. They took him away and they held her while she cried out. But though she tore her hair, they would not let her go near. The Priest said she must keep away. For the sake of her small daughter, he said, she must not go near, must keep herself apart. Many people listened now to the Priest. He sent for powerful medicines and a magic glass to scrape the skin. He gave the medicine only to those who were well, her daughter the first among them, and the others he placed in his church to live or to die as the Lord Above decreed. But the Priest's power was not complete. When the Girl asked him as she did everyday if the child would be safe he could not answer.

# THE OLD WOMAN

Darkness drip from the trees
Rain
Rain down in the deep holes
Rain down on the boxes
Under the earth
Darkness cover all my power
Old men old women
Lovers
Little children
Gone
All gone into darkness
Under the earth
No food for the journey
Dirt in their mouths
No clothes
No blankets
Only words
To freeze their souls
All burned
To burn away the plague
Smell of smoke in my nostrils as I die
Smell of the lives of my people burning
Being burned
By the foolish priest

Dangerous priest
Now you give you take
Believe you have everything
With your magic glass
Power of life power of death
No
Only the living are beholden
No priest have power
Over the dead
In their resting place
How my spirit call to them
Take me
Take me to you
Let no priest take my body
They my people they
Will take me
Make them swear to take me
To the burial ground
Make them

## THE GIRL

Such a tiny box they made for her daughter and such a big hole under the earth. The Father-not-father told them how it should be done.

And all our doing? Ah, no. I cannot think about it.

# V

## THE PRIEST

*2³RD JUNE   Sent a week ago to Nanaimo where I hear the soldiers have more vaccine. We did not escape the reach of the smallpox here. Indeed I fear we may have brought it back with us for the man who came back with me was the first to succumb. I have done my best to stem the spread of the disease with vaccine obtained from HMS Vantage in Barkley Sound. Nevertheless, thirty-five have so far fallen victim, including the old woman, whose imminent death is having a most depressing effect on the others.*

And the girl's infant. No miracle when I asked for one. Dear God, the poor girl.

The old woman lingers. In a way, she brought it on herself. She kept her distance when it all began, watching me while I went to each case, cursing me no doubt. When the vaccine arrived she denounced me for Chigha, the Evil One, refused point blank to be touched. But when the disease was at its height she was there, working beside me.

The girl's husband went down with it—the Beautiful Boy with his head and hands all purpled and swollen with running sores, his eyes closed to slits—and she was there, then, helping. I told her not to, said only if she was vaccinated, but she wouldn't listen. She took the rag from me and went over to his mat. Began sponging the terrible face. Touching. With her bony hands.

After that what did it matter? She came with me to every case, even the worst. We moved all the victims into the church and she set up her fire there, burning shreds of bark, filling the church with its smoke. She kept the families of the sick away. Some of them, the girl with her infant among them, refused. I had vaccinated the child along with the others. They stayed outside the church, chanting sometimes, sometimes drumming. And I prayed.

It was not much to ask. A small life.

When we put the child's coffin in the ground today she asked me why, and I had no answer. God gives me no answer. I said the plague was sent by God because we do not follow his ways. But a newborn child? Can I ask her, any of them, to believe in this Father? Love such a Father?

"I will pray," she said.

"You cannot go in to the Church."

"No," she said. "Not in the Church."

I let her go and then I followed her. I didn't want another disappearance on my hands. We are few enough, God knows.

She went up to the burial ground. A pagan temple of trees on the rock, the sunlight pouring through the cedars. If there had been time enough I swear I would have gone up there too, to pray for the souls I had buried in the dirt. Who to confess that to? A priest praying in a heathen place. Would it be the worst sacrilege?

The old woman will be next. It is exactly fifteen days from the time when she touched the terrible face. I knew straight away. And so did she. I have taken it

from him she said. And I could almost believe—God
forgive me—because he has recovered. Weak certainly,
but the fever is all gone and the inflammation, the skin
calmer, and he can see. Now she lies in his place, blind
and in pain.

*All time now is taken with caring for the sick. Please God*
*we can stem the tide.*

## THE GIRL

When the Girl's child was buried under the ground according to the word of the Father-not-father, the Girl left her husband and her sick grandmother and took herself away in the way of her people to the Burial Ground to fast there and to pray. It was on the fourth day of her fasting that she found the skull and some small bones to which some withered shreds still clung. She picked up the skull. Large it was, like a moon in summer, large and round and crazed with a tracery of madness and of love. Then she began to know. The moon in her hands, hollow with wanting, filled with knowledge. No magic and no conjuring tricks. There had been no magic. Ever. Only a brief struggle in the darkness. Like a loving or a birth. Or a kiss. And the bones returned to their place. The Priest had no magic in his words or in his hands. And no more was he responsible for a life than for a death. Slowly she rocked, cradling the knowledge.

When her retreat was over, the Girl returned to the village and went straight to her husband, the Beautiful Boy, not sure what she would say to him, or do. She found him sleeping, with his face turned up, all unaware, and her heart turned in pity, like a fish on a line. For here was no more finery or flash of sun on feather, no more swooping to love.

She took his rough face in her hands, laid her cheek on his and spoke skin through skin of love and loving and tenderest forgiveness. Then she felt his body wanting, asking for sweetness, and she gave it.

Then, now, she could give it. While you need, while you hurt. There, touch, take. I give all that you want. It is yours. And the tears that slide from under your eyelids, mine to take. To drink. And my tears for you, falling, while we fall, while we fall, while we love.

## THE PRIEST

*1ST JULY   News today that the neighbouring village across the inlet is stricken with the smallpox. Our cases, praise God, seem fewer. Buried the old woman yesterday and two others. There have been none since.*

Buried her in the ground we have set aside. What else could I do? She had me to her on her death bed. The others were afraid, glad to be told to stay away. "Listen, Priest," she said. She reached out and clawed at my arm. She couldn't see any more. "Not in the ground," she said. "Not like the others. Make them take me to the Burial Ground," she said. "Make them." I couldn't answer her. She hauled herself up off her cot then and began to shriek. "Make them! Make them!" I had no choice. I had to say it, had to say yes to quieten her. Yes I promise. But when it was over I dug her grave. What else could I do? Leave her out there? A smallpox victim? To reinfect the village? What's left of it.

*With the help of the medical supplies from the fort, I think we have turned the tide. Tomorrow we must burn all the clothing and bedding and with it I pray the last of the infection. Tomorrow I may go across the inlet to help them there. They have nothing.*

And see it all again? As if the first time were not enough to teach the hardest lesson of all—that it is not for us even to ask, still less to understand. Watch it all happen again? And not question? Pray again and know now not to ask for miracles? Accept it all? Thy will be done?

## POOR-BABY-THOMAS

the girl came with her hands warm to my face      with
love  pouring  in  the  hollow  places      filling  the
emptiness      the      dark      with      light      and
another      not the girl      nor yet the one with the
beautiful  face but  another      who was not of the
people      who  came dressed in a dark robe      who
came  with  cool  white  hands      prying  fingers  and
hard  thumbs      tracing  a  curious  path  across  my
forehead      round      the      hollows      of      my
eyes      searching      look i˙said      look and i will
show you all i have to show      over and over then in
the  cool  hands      the  fingers  searching  out  and
finding      learning all the paths of love      then tears
trickling  hot through the cracks      melting away the
crust  of  reproach      the  layers  of  guilt  and
blame      until  they  knew      and were still      and
returned me to the leaf and the dark      the soft black
bed of mold      to be tumbled by the spears of new
green

## THE PRIEST

5 TH AUGUST   *Returned here yesterday somewhat*
*apprehensive at the prospect of facing the destruction*
*that was caused last month by the fire, but anxious*
*nevertheless to assess the damage and see what, if anything,*
*might be done about it. Our church, it is my sad duty to*
*report, was all but destroyed when some of the villagers*
*assisting with the burning of the clothes & bedding*
*inadvertently set fire to the timbers. Before we knew it the*
*blaze was out of control. There was little that we could do*
*but watch and pray although some brave fellows made a*
*desperate attempt to beat out the flames with boughs they*
*hacked from the nearest trees. The accident occurred on the*
*morning I was to leave for the stricken village across the*
*inlet. Overcome with shock at the grievous occurrence, I*
*naturally deferred my departure although my continued*
*presence was of dubious benefit, the Indians having fallen*
*to bickering among themselves over who was to blame.*
*Greatly discouraged I at last retired to the forest where I*
*made my own peace.*

*The next morning I set out as planned to the village*
*across the inlet where they had a hard time of it and where*
*the disease dealt a final bitter blow, taking victim the good*
*fellow who accompanied me to help.*

*Although we remained at the settlement as long as we could be of use, few there received us without misgivings, most showing great resistance and suspecting some connection between us and the old woman, whose memory they seemed to fear. Some, however, let me help them and I did what I could.*

And came home. Paddling across water so clear you could see the fish. The imprint of the skull on the palms of my hands, its words inside my skull, all the words that cannot be spoken, only heard through skin, through bone. No sound but the hollow slap of the paddle on the flat surface. The shore sliding closer. The bare ribs of the church up there on the rise standing out black against the bright blue.

The village was all but deserted. Most of them were out gathering clams, bent like slow beetles stranded at the water's edge. Only the girl and her husband came to meet me. No cradle board on her back. There was a great expanse of mud (even the mud blue, with the sky shining in the shallow puddles), and the tide was lower than I have seen it for a long while.

He helped me bring the canoe up.

"Father-not-father?"

I knew what he wanted to say.

"You must go to the Burial Ground," he said.

"No. There's nothing for me there."

"But—" he stopped, the canoe heavy between us with the weight of the unsaid words.

"No," I said again. I have seen your sin in all its pity. It is the same as mine. "Let him rest undisturbed. Where he belongs."

He looked at me sharply, knowing that I knew, not knowing how. Ready to run.

"Come on," I said.

*On my arrival here, the sight of the church with its disfigured timbers was most poignant. There seems to be little hope of rebuilding until the remaining villagers are fully recuperated and their spirits revived. In the meantime I shall assist the people in their daily tasks. Until work is resumed, then, this entry in the record of the progress of the mission shall constitute the last.*

# VI

## THE GIRL

The early mist still clings to the rock—though it is summer—like a wreath of winter breath. Up here past the still pool is the forbidden place. No one now to bid or forbid. And if there was I should not listen. I thought the Father-not-father was afraid to come but he is up ahead, bending to the pull of the climb. And why should he be afraid? The Great Rock cannot harm him. There is no Power in the rock any more than there is a Shining Man on the water. Was there a Power to hear the prayers of my Grandmother, to listen to the prayers of the Priest? Poor-Baby-Thomas given to the darkness. My kingfisher's fire turned to cinders. My daughter, my swallow, in a deep hole under the earth. No. I will not believe in a Power that can do these things. All these years upon years, all these lives upon lives have my people prayed to the Power, yearned for the Power, died for the Power. All these years upon years have they listened to the tales. But the tales come from the curled lips of dead men and are empty.

The Power is all the time inside us and the tales we tell are to hide its terrible face. Nor do I believe the Priest and his Forever. Look at the sea. Still as a windless day and shining like the skin of a salmon. The sky above is the same blue, pale and luminous. The sky is

light itself. The sea the shadow of this light. It is beautiful. All across the silky skin of the sea lie the long thin
ridges of the waves, pleating one into another, into another, countless. Forever is now. Not in the time that
was before nor in the time to come. All the life there is
is here on the mountain, now, under this summer
morning. There is only the summer morning. And it is
enough. I shall not ask for more. All that is given is
taken away. I shall not ask again.

The mist thins, lifts. The sun shafts in on us as we
climb. It whitens the rock, warms the stone. The day is
new. I will not have a past. I want none. Only today
and what there is now. Nothing more.

## THE PRIEST

"Come up to the Great Rock," she said. She stood in what was once the doorway of our church, between the charred timbers. "Come up with me. Your Shining Man will not come to hear you pray in this place. It is like a skeleton."

"God is everywhere," I said.

"Then come up to the Great Rock," she said.

So here I am, almost at the top. And out of breath. How small it looks down there. The cross of yellow cedar. Weathered already, greying. Melting into the beach, the trees. How the forest takes it all back. Like the burial place, somewhere over there where the trees hesitate before the cliff. From up here no sign of the bones of the dead who have gone before. Hidden in the trees. But there all the same, with power enough to make a murderer confess. I could have him now, and he'd be hanged. No doubt about it. It would be the proper thing to do. And all the proper ladies in Victoria would applaud, celebrate the prosecution of a nefarious criminal, commend the moral rectitude and steadfast resolve of the watchful priest. Oh, yes. It would be the proper thing. And yes, my name would be vindicated against the vile lies he put about, striding up and down the beach that day, the fur blanket, the poor baby's blanket, like a flag overhead: *The Priest. It is the Priest's doing. He must make amends.*

How long ago it seems. And how unimportant. And yet I did consider. Alone among the trees, the shape of innocence lying at my feet. The proper thing was obvious. Take the bones. Confront the girl's husband. Have him escorted to Victoria for trial. Lay to rest the child's remains, at last. In consecrated ground. The Christian bones in a Christian place. Dust to dust. My sacred duty and my duty to my Queen fulfilled. I picked up the skull, began to look, turned it over. And the world turned backwards on itself, unwinding everything that had gone before. Down there in the deep quiet and the dark shadows, I could hear, I could see. I held the distorted skull a long time. Listened to the unraveling of sorrow.

He lies there for the old woman, for them all. May perpetual light shine upon them.

I shall not disturb him now. The burned out church, the longhouse, the boats abandoned like empty seed pods on the beach—they will all come and go. But the bones will always be there, cradled in the tall trees. Rattling against each other when a storm blows. Bleaching the dark.

PAULINE HOLDSTOCK was born in England and graduated from London University in English, French, and history. She taught in England, the Bahamas, and Canada, and now lives in British Columbia.

Her first novel, *The Blackbird's Song*, was a finalist in the W.H. Smith / *Books in Canada* First Novel Award, 1987. Her short stories have appeared in *Exile, Event, Grain, NeWest Review, Malahat Review, Flare, Antigonish Review*, and *New Quarterly*.